STAN
Mystery
Series

MULTICULTURAL READERS
SET 2

AS THE
EAGLE GOES

ANNE SCHRAFF

Artesian Press

P.O. Box 355 Buena Park, CA 90621

STANDING TALL MYSTERY SERIES
MULTICULTURAL READERS
SET 2

Project Editor: Carol E. Newell
Cover Illustrator: Fujiko
Cover Design: Tony Amaro
©2000 Artesian Press

ISBN 1-58659-086-

Chapter 1

As Jim Black Eagle raced up the hill he was surprised how easy it was getting. He was building his strength. He felt good about this Saturday's meet. South of here, way back in 1912 before Jim's grandfather was born, another young Native American ran to glory. He was James Francis Thorpe, or Bright Path, his tribal name. Thorpe was from the Sac tribe, but Jim was Lakota Sioux.

"You'll be the next Native American to win Olympic gold," Grandfather said. He was seventy now, and he often told Jim of how much he admired Thorpe.

Jim enjoyed running, but he didn't know if he'd ever be good enough to dream of Olympic gold. Jim's father would have been good enough but he was injured in his Air Force trainer while still a young man. Now he worked from a wheelchair and also dreamed of Jim fulfilling his own promise.

"Run for your father," Grandfather said. "Run for the honor of the Lakota Sioux."

Jim Black Eagle was named for Jim Thorpe, but he wanted to run only for himself. He wanted to run for the sheer joy of it and if he won anything, that was frosting on the cake. But everybody else, including Coach Schultz, had their own goals for him.

Jim was at the top of the hill when he saw the car coming. It seemed to be coming right at him, and he jumped into the brush alongside the road. Only as the passing car rocked with laughter did Jim recognize his old enemy, Travis Lansing.

"Cluck, cluck, cluck goes the chicken," Travis yelled. "Hope you didn't sprain your ankle, Black Eagle. I hope you didn't land in a bed of rattlesnakes!"

Jim brushed himself off, unhurt and glared after the vanishing car. He hadn't jumped into the brush because he was a coward—it was the sensible thing to do. But now he saw it was only part of Lansing's campaign to rattle his nerves before Saturday.

If any boy from Santo Cristobal's track team advanced to the next competition, it would be Travis or Jim. Jim held the best time so far—he had run the metric mile in 4:18.76. His goal was to run it in less than four minutes. Travis' best time was 4:19.49. Travis figured he didn't have a chance to beat Jim's time unless Jim ran Saturday well below his personal best.

Jim continued jogging towards Santo Cristobal High School, letting his resentment against Lansing burn off in the exercise. It wasn't only that Travis was his fiercest competitor, but he played dirty.

Travis Lansing didn't know how to play on an even field. He knew better than to try any funny business at the track meet itself. But when nobody was watching he pulled out all the stops. He once told Jim to study the wrong chapter in a test. He hoped Jim would flunk Biology and be too upset to do his best in a meet. Or just before a meet he'd make ugly comments about Jim's heritage, hoping he could break Jim's concentration.

Jim saw the school in the distance, a group of one-story buildings lying in the valley in the shadow of hills. It wasn't a large school but Jim thought it was a good place. The class Jim enjoyed most was Art. He loved to paint in oils—big, bold action scenes of his ancestors riding spirited horses over the plains. The art teacher, Amy Beldanes was a fine artist herself. She had art shows in Santa Fe, New Mexico.

Jim had art class first and he walked into the classroom with his usual pride. His paintings were often displayed on the walls. Now, he saw a girl admiring his painting of a warrior on a white horse against a fiery sky. She smiled at Jim and said, "It's marvelous!"

"Thanks, Sasha," Jim said, blushing a little. He sat at his desk and pulled open the drawer where he kept his art supplies. There he found a crude drawing of a comic Indian lying prone on the ground. *Remember, Custer's side won in the end*, was scrawled across the drawing.

Chapter 2

Jim bunched up the paper and threw it in the trash.

"What was that?" Sasha asked.

"A stupid note from a jerk," Jim snapped. "Nothing to worry about."

Sasha smiled. "You're going to be in the track and field prelims next Saturday, aren't you, Jim?"

"Yeah," Jim said, still thinking about the ugly note.

"If you're in the top nine you get to go to the finals. Wow, you could be in the finals and be a State champion, Jim," Sasha said.

"Lots of great runners from the other schools are coming," Jim said. "Last year Santo Cristobal had four runners in the finals, but this year we'll maybe have two."

"I'll bet you run better because Lansing is pushing you, huh?" Sasha said.

"Maybe so," Jim admitted, "but he'd like to push me right into the Missouri River."

Ms. Beldanes came into the classroom then. She wasn't wearing her usual happy smile. "Before we get to work," she said, "I'm very sorry to have to tell you that I was robbed yesterday."

"Robbed?" a girl gasped.

"Yes. I had four of my best paintings stolen from my car. I left them for about five minutes in an unlocked car. When I returned they were gone. It's a great loss to me. I had painted them for a man in Santa Fe who was going to pay me a thousand dollars for them," Ms. Beldanes said.

Everybody looked at each other. "Who'd steal your desert paintings, Ms.

Beldanes?" Jodie Neal asked. "I mean where would they sell them out here?"

"Yeah," Sasha agreed. "I wouldn't know how to begin to sell art like that."

"I'm not sure who would do such a thing. I only know that it was someone in this school. No strangers were around at the time. I'm deeply, deeply hurt. If any of you learn anything about this, please let me know. If someone in this class took the paintings, for whatever reason, I beg you to just return them and no questions will be asked. Just leave them in my classroom after school and you won't get into any trouble, I promise you," Ms. Beldanes said.

"You think somebody in *this* class took them?" Jim asked.

"I hate to think so. The paintings were only displayed in this class. Only students from here could have seen me put them in my car. The paintings were wrapped in canvas. Someone just glancing in the car wouldn't have known what they were."

Jim looked around at his fourteen fellow art students. It didn't seem any of *them* would do such a thing.

After class, Jim walked out with Riley Bennett, a skinny kid who was also on the track team though he was a mediocre runner.

"Boy, Riley, what a lousy thing to happen to Ms. Beldanes!" Jim said.

"Yeah," Riley agreed, "and she's my best teacher. My other teachers are just going through the motions. But she cares. She's so nice, and pretty, too."

Jim nodded. Ms. Beldanes was about thirty with long, black hair and dusky skin. "I wish I could help her get her paintings back," Jim said.

"Yeah," Riley said. "Me, too!"

Later, as Jim and Riley ate lunch, Travis Lansing came strolling by. "Hey, Injun," he yelled at Jim, "did you steal the art teacher's paintings? It's all over school that somebody took them. I guess stealing is just in your bones, huh? You people just don't understand you can't take stuff that doesn't belong to you."

Jim stood, glaring at Travis. "Don't talk to me about stealing, Lansing. Your ancestors took what belonged to my ancestors a long time ago, okay?" Jim snapped. "So if thieving is in somebody's bones, maybe it's your bones!"

Chapter 3

"Touché," laughed Sasha, who was sitting nearby. "That's a good one, Jim."

Lansing decided to change the subject. "How're the legs feeling, Jim? That tendonitis you had last year in your Achilles tendon coming back? Remember how it kept you out of the finals last year?" Lansing said.

"I'm feeling terrific—at the top of my game," Jim snapped. "I'll wipe you out Saturday. You'll be eating my dust."

"I don't know," Lansing said, "you might just wake up in the morning and there it is, pain. Man, just think about all that pain and trying to run with it."

"Get lost, Lansing. You're getting

old," another boy said.

Jim went on to his Physics class where he was struggling, and then History, which he didn't like much. He finished the day in English where he was hanging on to a C+. His only really good classes were Art and PE.

After school, Jim ran some laps around the stadium and he noticed Sasha sitting in the stands which were otherwise empty. "Poetry in motion," she said when he stopped where she sat.

"That's nice," Jim said. "You're nice."

"You are, too, Jim. I love to watch you run. It's so smooth. I'm a clumsy athlete. I play softball but it's not a pretty sight." Sasha turned then and said, "Look, there's Riley Bennett helping Ms. Beldanes carry her art equipment. He's really crazy about her, poor guy. He told me that since she was robbed he's appointed himself her unofficial bodyguard so nothing else bad happens to her."

Jim laughed. Then he saw Travis begin to do laps around the track. Travis looked awfully fast. Maybe, Jim thought, he'd gotten good enough to beat anybody! If the other schools sent terrific speedster, Jim could just miss making the final nine. He wouldn't even go to the finals then.

Jim could see his grandfather's face hanging with disappointment. It was Grandfather who helped Mom raise Jim. Grandfather took Jim canoeing and taught him how to fish and use a rifle. He taught Jim a hundred other things as well—honesty, manliness, fairness, the beauty and grandeur of his heritage, and pride in himself. Jim's father taught him courage.

Jim didn't want to let grandfather down by not making it into the finals. "Lansing looks fast, huh, Sasha?" Jim asked.

"Yeah, but you're faster," Sasha said.

"I don't know. Last time we competed he was breathing down my neck!" Jim said.

Lansing stopped where Jim and Sasha were. "I hear two guys from Southwest are real speed demons. Canyon has three fireballs, too, and Bouquet and Arroyo both got good runners. Monte Blanco has a good guy. That leaves one spot for a guy from Santo Cristobal and I'm planning on being in the finals, Jim," Lansing said.

"Dream on, Lansing," Jim said.

"Look, Indian boy, you still have your art. You can still paint pretty pictures of the days when the Indians ruled the land," Lansing said in a mocking tone.

"Lansing, go find a bucket of water the janitor is using to clean the johns and stick your head in it, okay?" Jim said.

"Uh-oh," Lansing said, "look who's coming this way with fire in her eyes— Ms. Beldanes. I bet she's coming to accuse you of stealing her pictures, Jim. You better start running."

Jim turned to see Ms. Beldanes walking briskly towards him. Could Lansing have lied about Jim to her? Did he accuse Jim of stealing her paintings? Would Lansing sink that low? Jim's legs turned numb.

"Jim Black Eagle," Ms. Beldanes said, "may I see you?"

Chapter 4

Jim walked over to a shady spot covered by a trellis. "Yeah, what's up, Ms. Beldanes?" he asked.

"I was so upset in class over my loss. I forgot to ask you if I could enter three of your paintings in the regional student art competition," Ms. Beldanes said.

Jim let out his breath in a long gasp of relief. "Sure. That'd be great."

"I think you have a good chance of winning scholarship money, Jim. I've seen the level of art in the regionals and yours is exceptional, even for an adult. You remind me of Joseph Turner—you have the same emotional, personal approach to nature," Ms.

Beldanes said.

"Thanks, Ms. Beldanes," Jim said, his heart pounding with excitement.

"If you win recognition in the regionals you might even get money for a summer in Europe," Ms. Beldanes said. Jim felt as if he were flying. He had the same joyous feeling he had when he was sprinting across the prairie competing only with the wind.

When Ms. Beldanes walked away, Jim returned to where Sasha and Lansing waited.

"So when are the police coming for you?" Lansing asked. "We'll all come visit you in jail. Maybe Sasha will bake a cake for you—with a saw in it so you can break out."

"Ms. Beldanes is entering three of my paintings in the regional competition," Jim told Sasha, ignoring Lansing completely.

"Oh, Jim! That's terrific," Sasha said, jumping up and giving Jim a big hug.

When Jim got home from school his father was working on his computer but Grandfather sat on the porch waiting for Jim. Jim sat down beside his grandfather and the old man said, "How is the training going for Saturday?"

"Good. I'm feeling strong," Jim said. "I got exciting news today, Grandfather. Three of my oil paintings are going to be in a big art competition."

Grandfather was silent for a few minutes, then he said, "When you were a small boy you drew wonderful pictures. But now you are almost a man. Drawing pictures is for children."

"Grandfather, you're a wise man. You've heard of great artists like Michelangelo and Rembrandt. I mean, Ms. Beldanes says I'm really good and I could maybe win a scholarship to study art in Europe," Jim said.

Grandfather's face hardened. "Men in this family do not make pictures.

Your father could run like a deer. He was a great athlete and so he named his son for Jim Thorpe. Your father was hurt in the airplane accident. Now he makes computers talk. But the dream that was in his heart must be fulfilled in you," he said.

"Yes, I know," Jim said. He'd heard the story often enough to know it by heart.

"A man's triumph is a triumph of strength," Grandfather continued, his voice almost angry. "They said of Jim Thorpe that trying to catch him when he ran was like trying to catch a shadow. In 1912 when I was not yet born, Thorpe won the decathlon and the pentathlon—the only time both events were won by the same man. He was the greatest athlete of the century or maybe of all time. He was a Sac tribesman."

"I know, Grandfather," Jim sighed.

"They stole his medals from him in

1913. They shamed him, just because he played baseball before the Olympic games. They shamed all of us by doing that. You will erase the shame, Jim. When they place the gold medal around your neck, then the shameful thing done to Jim Thorpe will be erased," Grandfather said.

Jim watched his father wheel into the room. Dad smiled at Jim and said softly, "Whatever you do with your life will make me proud, son."

But Grandfather said firmly, "You were born to triumph as a runner, not a painter!"

Chapter 5

"Don't mind Grandfather," Mom said as she put on dinner. "It's wonderful and exciting that you're such an excellent artist, Jim."

"Thanks, Mom. Grandfather figures I could be the greatest artist on earth. But if I don't win Saturday, and then in the finals and on to the Olympics, I've betrayed the spirit of Jim Thorpe! He really wants me to win," Jim groaned.

"Oh, he's an old man. He's lost in his dreams, Jim," Mom said.

But Jim wanted Grandfather to be proud of him. He wanted that more than anything.

Early the next day at school, Jim saw a boy named Nazario lurking around the art room. He wasn't one of Ms. Beldanes students so why was he sneaking around where she kept the art supplies in the little shed behind her classroom?

"Hey, look, Riley," Jim said to his friend, "what's Nazario doing over there? I better check it out."

"Let me handle it," Riley said. He strode over to the shed and talked to Nazario for a few minutes, then he came back. "It's okay, Jim. Nazario had Ms. Beldanes permission to borrow some red paint for a poster. Uh, when anything looks fishy, Jim, just tell me. I'm like Ms. Beldanes special protector now."

"Oh," Jim said. "Then it's possible you'll find her lost paintings, too, huh?"

"You bet. I'm working on that. I expect to get the paintings back for her real soon," Riley said.

Jim grinned at Riley. "Are you a detective or what? I mean, I don't get it."

"I've been working real hard on clues and stuff, Jim. I'm ready to crack the case. I figure Ms. Beldanes will be mighty grateful when I find her paintings."

"Sure, Riley ..." Jim said.

"Jim, how old do you figure she is?" Riley asked.

"Oh ... thirty maybe," Jim said.

"Thirty? She's not thirty! I know what thirty looks like. Ms. Beldanes is about twenty-two."

"Well, she's been teaching here for five years, Riley. Before that, she taught at Arroyo. She must've been fifteen years old when she started teaching," Jim said, laughing.

"Well, maybe she's like twenty-six or something," Riley said. "That means she's not even ten years older than me."

Jim was shocked. "What're you getting at, Riley?"

"Well, I'm almost an adult and

maybe she'll want to go out with me," Riley said.

"Oh, man," Jim said, "don't be stupid! They hang teachers by their thumbs if they get social with kids!"

Riley gave Jim a dirty look and stalked off.

Jim didn't want to overtrain for Saturday, so he took it easy on Thursday and Friday. Early Saturday morning the bus pulled into the school grounds and the track team from Santo Cristobal piled on. There was a big group of sprinters, runners, and hurdlers from the school.

Travis Lansing slipped in beside Jim on the bus. Jim felt like complaining to Coach Schultz about his seat-mate, but the coach hated hassles so Jim decided to grin and bear it.

"Do you believe in horoscopes?" Lansing asked.

"No," Jim said.

"Well, mine said today is my big

day. I looked yours up, too. It said be prepared for disappointment," Lansing said.

"I'm already disappointed over who's sitting next to me," Jim snapped.

"Any sign of your tendonitis, Indian boy?" Lansing asked.

Jim stared at the beautiful rock formations flying by the bus windows. When he had some free time, he'd paint them. "Go bust a rock with your head, Lansing," he said.

Chapter 6

When the bus came to a stop, the team filed off in the bright sunlight. They had been beaten to the stadium by some fans, including Jim's grandfather. His red pickup truck was already parked in the visitors lot.

When the competitors walked into the stadium, Jim glanced at the stands. He saw his grandfather and half a dozen other Sioux men with sun darkened, well-lined serious faces. Grandfather had come prepared for a celebration. Jim hoped he could deliver.

When the 1600 meter event came up, Jim walked confidently to the starting line. All the boys got on their marks, got set and leaped forward at the signal. Coach Schultz had urged the boys to train hard, but at the same time he always said runners were born, not made. The speed was bred in their bones.

A boy from Arroyo was out in front and then two speedsters from Southwest followed. Jim ran his own race, not even looking at his competition. He knew Travis was close on his heels as he overtook the Southwest runners and edged past the boy from Arroyo. Jim knew he was beating his own personal best in this race. He felt airborne as he ran away from the others and flew through the finish line to the rising screams from the stands. Jim could swear he heard the gruff, gravelly voice of Grandfather above all the others chanting,

"Go Jim Black Eagle!"

When the times were posted it was a new record for the field prelims. Jim had run the 1600 meters in four minutes 7.52 seconds. He could see the fans jumping up and down as flashbulbs popped. No boy from this area had even come close to running such a fast race.

Travis Lansing also made the finals but at a disappointing, for him, four minutes, 24 seconds. He only survived the semis because the other boys ran well behind their own personal bests.

A reporter from the local paper did an on-the-spot interview with Jim and took some more pictures of him. "You'll be page one on the sports page tomorrow, kid," the reporter promised.

Jim finally made his way back to the bus. The other team members slapped him on the back, congratulating him, all but Lansing who sat as far away as he could on the bus.

"You put Santo Cristobal on the map, Jim," Coach Schultz said on the bus ride back to school. "We've never had a boy run the 1600 meters in your time. I think you stand a good chance of breaking the four minute barrier in the finals. I think you're primed for it. A kid ran it in 3:59.9 in 1966 and Jim Ryan and Marty Lipman broke it in 1965."

Back at school, Jim's parents, Grandfather, and the old men he brought with him waited with hugs and praise. "All I did was win a race," Jim laughed, but he enjoyed all the excitement.

The write-up in the paper featured a dramatic action shot of Jim crossing the finish line. *Sioux runner revives ghost of Jim Thorpe,* cried the headline. The story told of Jim's background, his dreams of being an artist; his father's triumph over crippling injuries. "It's a beautiful story," Mom said, her eyes wet. "I'm getting copies of the article so I can mail them to everyone I know!"

"It's good how they tell that you are Lakota Sioux," Grandfather said. "But remember, Jim, your heart is only big enough for one dream. Put the artist idea aside and follow your true goal— the Olympic gold."

Jim said nothing. He didn't want to spoil this wonderful day. Later he had a date with Sasha. He was anxious to pick her up in Grandfather's red pickup truck and take her to a nice place to eat.

As Jim closed the door for Sasha and ran around to the other side of the truck to drive away, a rock crashed into his windshield.

"What the ..." he cried furiously, staring around in the darkness.

Chapter 7

Jim saw nobody, but he had a pretty good idea of who threw the rock. Travis Lansing was really bitter since the prelims. He was even telling people that Jim somehow put a curse on him with the help of a local medicine man and that's why he didn't run as fast as he had before.

Jim's windshield looked like a spider's web with a tiny indentation where the rock hit surrounded by crooked lines going off in all directions. "Creep!" Jim muttered as he got in. "I'd like to meet him and whip him good."

"Oh, Jim," Sasha said, "the finals are next Saturday. It would be stupid to risk an injury just to settle a score with a worthless jerk like Lansing."

"I guess. But, man, does it mean that much to him to win? It doesn't even mean that much to me. If it wasn't for Grandfather I might not even be competing. I'd be out running on the prairie for the fun of it. Why does it mean so much to Lansing?"

Sasha shook her head. "I don't know. It's sorta in the air—some little voice that tells us all that winning is just about everything. But we never find out why."

They drove to a new little Greek restaurant and had chicken rice pilaf. You could see the mountains in the moonlight from a big picture window.

"It looks like something you might've painted, Jim," Sasha said.

"Hah. Nothing looks as good as the real thing," Jim said.

At school on Tuesday, Ms. Beldanes was ecstatic. "My paintings were returned!" she announced to the class.

"One of our own students found them for me!"

Jim glanced over at Riley who was grinning proudly. Ms. Beldanes continued, "Riley Bennett tracked them down to an empty store in town where the thief had stashed them. It's simply amazing that Riley was able to work on a few clues and find my paintings! I just can't thank him enough!"

Riley grinned more widely as the class applauded.

"Hey, fantastic, man," Jim told Riley as they walked out together. "I gotta be honest—I didn't think you could find the paintings."

Riley laughed. "I've always loved detective stories. I've read every Sherlock Holmes."

"Did you find out who ripped the paintings off?" Jim asked.

"No. But the important thing was getting them back. Hey, Jim, how was that little Greek restaurant where you took Sasha? Was it great?" Riley asked.

"Uh, yeah, the food was good and the views, too ..." Jim said, puzzled.

"Was Sasha impressed?" Riley asked.

"Uh, sure ... but ..."

"That's where I'm taking Amy," Riley said.

"Amy? Amy? You mean Ms. Beldanes?" Jim gasped.

"She's Amy to me now," Riley said. "I'm going to ask her right now."

"Don't do it, Riley," Jim pleaded. "She's a teacher and you're a student and it'll just embarrass her."

"You're just jealous you didn't get to do her a big favor like I did," Riley exploded into sudden anger. "Eat your heart out, Jim Black Eagle! I'm going to date the most beautiful teacher in the west!"

Jim shook his head and walked towards his next class. When he saw Lansing he stopped. "Look, the next rock that anybody throws at my window is going to be crammed down that jerk's throat, get it?" Jim said.

"I don't know what you're talking about," Lansing said.

"Just make sure there's no second time, man," Jim said.

"You think you're big stuff, don't you, Indian boy? Well, just because you finished up front once doesn't mean it'll happen again. Next time you'll be eating my dust and the Eagle will be drooping!" Lansing said.

Jim went to his desk and sat down. He couldn't figure out what demons were driving Travis. He made decent grades. His Dad wasn't one of those pushy guys who demand the best from their sons. Why was winning so important to him?

After class, Jim walked alongside Travis. "Tell me something, Lansing. Why is it so important for you to beat me Saturday? Why do you have to be the best runner around?" he asked.

Lansing turned to him, his eyes narrowing. "I want to win because I deserve to win. If it wasn't for you, then I'd be the star runner at Santo Cristobal. Why should some stupid Indian kid beat me at my own game?"

"I feel sorry for you, Lansing. You're a total jerk and you don't even know it. You're a spoiled little kid who wants the biggest candy cane in the store window, just because," Jim said.

As Jim walked away he saw Riley Bennett walking towards the art room. He had a bunch of flowers in his hand. He gripped the flowers and marched towards the art room. "Poor guy," Jim muttered to himself. "Poor guy."

Chapter 8

Late Tuesday Jim was walking towards the track for a few laps when he saw the lights still burning in Ms. Beldanes's classroom. She had driven away an hour ago, and she forgot to turn the lights off. Jim walked over to the janitor's office and they both returned to Ms. Beldanes's room to check.

"By golly," the janitor cried, "what a mess! Looks like she left in a big hurry. Papers scattered all over the floor. What a mess. And she's usually so neat."

Jim felt a bolt of fear go through him. He saw her small sports car leaving the faculty parking lot in a burst of speed. He thought she was driving kind of recklessly. He hadn't really seen her at the wheel—he just assumed she was driving. But now he had second thoughts. Maybe that fool Riley Bennett had gone off the deep end. Maybe he'd freaked and kidnapped her or something!

"Better check if Ms. Beldanes is okay," Jim said. "She was driving kind of funny when she left."

Mr. Dean, the school principal, immediately called Ms. Beldanes's home. She was at home, but she was very upset. She had a terrible scene with a hysterical student who had what she called a "fantasy" about her. She was all right and resting now.

Jim was relieved to hear that Ms. Beldanes was okay and he started to jog towards home. He felt sorry for poor Riley Bennett. He had no friends at school. He must have been really wiped out when Ms. Beldanes made him face the truth.

As Jim headed home, a car slowed down beside him. "Riley!" Jim gasped, recognizing the beat-up sedan.

"I gotta see you," Riley said. He looked pale and shaken. His face was bathed in perspiration. He got out of the car and said, "Will you drive, Jim? I'm real shaky. I just gotta talk."

Jim nodded, sliding under the wheel.

"She made me feel like a slime bug," Riley said.

"I'm sorry, man," Jim said softly. "Where do you want to go?"

"Out to the red rocks," Riley said.

Jim was driving north when he felt something sharp, like a gun, poking into his side. "Riley! What the ..." he cried.

"I know what's going on, Black Eagle," Riley hissed. "You pretended to be my friend, then you stabbed me in the back! You're in love with her, too! She loves you! That's why she made me feel like dirt!"

"Riley, you're nuts! She's just another teacher to me!" Jim said.

"You don't fool me anymore! She picked your paintings for that competition. She smiles at you! I'm not blind! But you got your pick of girls. You got Sasha and last year Desiré. I never had a girlfriend. You knew how much trouble I went to so Amy would like me. I stole her paintings just so I could find them for her, so she'd be grateful. Then I ask her out and she makes me feel like a slime bug! I didn't get it until Travis told me what was going on," Riley said.

"*Travis?*" Jim gasped.

"Yeah! I was coming out of her classroom. I told him what happened, and he explained it all." Riley jabbed Jim's ribs with the sharp object. "Travis told me how you and Ms. Beldanes laughed together about me and said I was a skinny nobody going nowhere.

Travis told me how you went behind my back and cut me down in Amy's eyes."

"That's a rotten lie," Jim cried.

"Travis said you liked Amy Beldanes a whole lot. And she likes you. He said Jim Black Eagle is a big shot who's an artist like her, so why should she give the time of day to a nobody like me?" Riley asked. "Well, you know what you did? You took away the only thing that mattered to me in the whole world. That's what you did."

Chapter 9

"Riley," Jim said, "Travis lied to you. I never talked to Ms. Beldanes about you. Don't you see what Travis is trying to do? He's trying to turn you against me, to make trouble for me so I can't beat him in the finals Saturday."

Riley kept pressing the object against Jim's side. "I don't believe you. Amy would've gone out with me. I know she would have. But you got to her. You have it all, and I got nothing!" Riley was crying now. "I think the world of her. I dream about her every night. Now my whole world has fallen apart. I can't even go back to school now, the way she shamed me!"

"Riley, you're not thinking straight.

What you need to do is go home and talk to your parents," Jim said.

"No!" Riley almost screamed. "I've shamed them, too! Amy is gonna tell them what a fool I made of myself. I even confessed to her that I stole her paintings, just so I could prove my love for her by giving them back. She'll send the cops after me now."

"No, she won't do that, Riley. She's a good person. She understands you just had a crush on her," Jim said. "Lots of guys fall into that trap with a pretty teacher."

"You're lying again. You're good at that!" Riley said. "Pull over right here."

Jim stopped the car and stared around at the mesas standing in the isolated area. "Riley, you're ruining your whole life," he warned.

"I don't care. It's ruined anyway. You took away the only good thing I ever had. Now get out of the car. I got a gun here, so don't try anything funny," Riley was breathing hard, gasping for air.

"Riley, what are you going to do?" Jim asked.

"Shut up!" Riley screamed. "Get moving up that trail ahead."

The trail wound around a spiral-shaped mountain. It was a rocky perilous path with a steep ascent. Riley kept close behind Jim, threatening him if he dared look back. "What are you trying to do, Riley?" Jim asked.

"Ruin it for you like you ruined it for me, Jim Black Eagle. I'm gonna destroy your dreams like you destroyed mine!" Riley snarled.

Cold chills went up Jim's spine. Riley Bennett was clearly in the grip of a terrible madness.

Chapter 10

Up and up the twisting trail they went, stopping at a place where the whole valley could be seen. A sea of reds and blues and greens swam before them. It was a beautiful sight, but Jim felt only terror.

"Now what, Riley?" Jim asked.

"Jump or I'll shoot you, Black Eagle," Riley said. "Your dream is running and winning the Olympics, but after you jump off the cliff you won't run any more!"

Jim stared down at the rocky cliffs below. He had just one choice. He had to fight Riley for the gun even at the risk of getting shot. No way was Jim going to jump off this mountain.

"Okay, Riley, if you say so," Jim said in as calm a voice as he could muster. As he spoke he whirled around and lunged at Riley, knocking the other boy down and almost over the edge. He grabbed Riley before he fell. Then he saw the object Riley threatened him with was not a gun at all. It was just a chunk of wood.

Riley lay sobbing on the trail. "Why don't you push me over, Black Eagle?" he wept. "Let the vultures have me. That's all I'm good for now. Vulture bait."

"Come on, Riley," Jim said. "We're walking back down. You're sick, real sick. But you'll get well. You'll be okay again, Riley, I promise you. And I'll still be your friend, because you didn't do all this bad stuff. It was your sickness making you act stupid."

Jim got Riley down the trail and back into the car. He drove directly to the Bennett house.

"Riley needs help," Jim told Mr. Bennett, who came out to the car.

"Yes," the man said, "Ms. Beldanes called and told us what happened. We've been out of our minds with worry."

"Thanks for bringing our son home, Jim," Mrs. Bennett said.

The last Jim saw of Riley was his parents gently leading him inside the house. Jim jogged over to Coach Schultz's house then and told him of Travis Lansing's part in turning Riley against him.

"He's always played dirty," Jim said, "but this time I think he's crossed the line."

"He won't be competing in the finals for Santo Cristobal this Saturday," the Coach said, "or ever. I'll talk to the principal about other disciplinary action."

On Saturday Jim Black Eagle ran a 1600 meter mile in 4:09.0 minutes.

Grandfather stood up and cheered with a yell that could be heard throughout the county. Tears ran down the old man's face, but for Jim the greatest moment came during the ride home with his grandfather.

"For me you have already won the Olympic gold, my grandson," Grandfather said. "Your father is proud of you. Your mother is proud of you. Jim Bright Path Thorpe smiles down upon you from the country of the Great Spirit. From now on, Jim Black Eagle, run for yourself or not at all."

Jim hugged his grandfather. It was the sweetest moment of his life. Even sweeter than when Ms. Beldanes told him he had won the regional art competition.

"My grandson, take up your jacket now and find your own path," Grandfather said.